Sue – Here's one to save & read to
your grandchildren. Hope you
enjoy it
            Mike

There's A Moose
On My Broomstick

By
Michael MacCurtain

Illustrated By Stan Jaskeil

Printed in Korea by asianprinting.com

ISBN 978-0-615-27511-6

About the Author:

Michael MacCurtain is a retired schoolteacher who wrote his first
Willie The Moose story for his students in Natick, Massachusetts.
He enjoys reading his stories to his own grandchildren.
He makes his home in Whitman, Massachusetts.

About the Illustrator:

Stan Jaskeil is a highly regarded illustrator. His work can be seen at his
website stanjaskielcartoons.com. He makes his home in Salem, Massachusetts and can be reached at
SJTOONS@aol.com

For:

Liam, Kaleigh, Seamus

Tara, Lia and Tony

The little ghosts and goblins of my Halloweens

May Willie's tricks be your Halloween treat

It was one of those gatherings in one of those places
Of strange looking women with warts on their faces.
They were wearing black capes and pointed black hats
And several were holding their own pretty black cats.
'Twas the pot they were stirring and their chanting so silly
That caught the attention of my good friend Willy.

For he'd stumbled that day in the Great North Wood
Upon a witches coven surely up to no good!
Yet it wasn't the witches or their bubbling brew,
What grabbed Willie's eyes were the brooms that they flew!

He'd seen them before on a cold Autumn night
As they flew cross the sky 'twas a very strange sight!
An old woman and a cat gliding high on a broom
Clearly lit up by a bright harvest moon,

And Willie would watch and remember the night
When Santa himself set Willie in flight
Over the country on that night he did soar,
Now all he wanted was to fly once more.

So he made up his mind, though it might mean his doom,
Our brave moose Willie would borrow a broom.

He watched and he studied as he returned each night
And he made his plans in spite of his fright.
He must be careful, quiet and quick
On the night he'd borrow Mafelda's broomstick.

For once he was off the witches would chase,
And if Willie should lose that terrible race,
There'd be no more North Woods for our brave Willie,
No…He'd be put in the pot where they'd boil him silly!

Yes Willie was certain he knew what they'd do
If they caught Willie they'd soon eat moose stew!

At the end of October, on a crisp autumn eve,
Ever so quietly our hero did weave
A Path through the North Woods where he had a date,
With a great new adventure that might seal his fate.
The witches were busy stirring their terrible brew
They never heard Willie as they boiled that stew.

Quiet and quick he grabbed for the broom,
Into the night he flew with a zoom!

As the best laid plans oft go awry,
There came a surprise as he started to fly.

As into the night he started to soar,
There came first a beep and then came a roar.
Who would have thought that a broom that was charmed
Would come equipped with a broomstick alarm!

Our Moose who'd planned to be a cool flying dude,
Was now a terrified moose being chased by a brood
Of witches so angry they'd give a lion a fright,
All Willie could do was race into the night!

Mafelda herself may have stayed on the ground
But Willie counted four other witches around!
He zigged and he zagged and he steered between trees,
When he looked back there were only three.
He lost two more o'er the Great North Woods lake
As he flew very low then gave a left fake!

Witch number four, though she tried her best,
Finally gave up and stopped for a rest.

Free from this posse Willie started to soar
As over the Northland he took a grand tour.

Over mountain and valley, up hillside and down,
Over the lakes and the rivers and over the towns.

He was coasting along towards morning's first light
When he suddenly beheld a very strange sight.
There on a fence post in black cape and hat
Softly weeping and alone old Mafelda she sat.
"A witch with no broom is as useless as rust,
By nighttime", said she, "I'll have turned all to dust"

Now our moose may be silly, but he's never unkind,
And did his best to keep that thought in mind.
"I was just having fun and I'm sorry you're sad"
Then he gave her the broom to make the witch glad.

Now, on autumn nights as you hear the winds moan,
Up in the North Woods standing alone,
Is one silly moose remembering his fright,
When he rode a witch's broomstick into the night!